♥ Mindy Kim
Makes a Splash! ♥

**Don't miss more fun adventures
with Mindy Kim!**

Mindy Kim

Makes a Splash!

BOOK
8

By Lyla Lee
Illustrated by Dung Ho

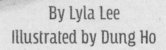

ALADDIN
New York London Toronto Sydney New Delhi

This book is a work of fiction. Any references to historical events, real people, or real places are used fictitiously. Other names, characters, places, and events are products of the author's imagination, and any resemblance to actual events or places or persons, living or dead, is entirely coincidental.

🦯 ALADDIN
An imprint of Simon & Schuster Children's Publishing Division
1230 Avenue of the Americas, New York, New York 10020
First Aladdin paperback edition July 2022
Text copyright © 2022 by Lyla Lee
Illustrations copyright © 2022 by Dung Ho
Also available in an Aladdin hardcover edition.
All rights reserved, including the right of reproduction in whole or in part in any form.
ALADDIN and related logo are registered trademarks of Simon & Schuster, Inc.
For information about special discounts for bulk purchases, please contact Simon & Schuster Special Sales at 1-866-506-1949 or business@simonandschuster.com.
The Simon & Schuster Speakers Bureau can bring authors to your live event. For more information or to book an event contact the Simon & Schuster Speakers Bureau at 1-866-248-3049 or visit our website at www.simonspeakers.com.
Designed by Laura Lyn DiSiena
The illustrations for this book were rendered digitally.
The text of this book was set in Haboro.
Manufactured in the United States of America 0522 OFF
10 9 8 7 6 5 4 3 2 1
Library of Congress Control Number 2022930396
ISBN 978-1-5344-8904-2 (hc)
ISBN 978-1-5344-8903-5 (pbk)
ISBN 978-1-5344-8905-9 (ebook)

To teachers of all kinds, who help us
learn new things and remind us to be
kinder to ourselves

Chapter 1

My name is Mindy Kim. I am nine years old, and I don't know how to swim.

I can splash around in shallow water and swim with floaties and inflatable tubes if I have to. But I never really learned how to *swim* swim. And I thought I wouldn't have to learn anytime soon . . . until one day we got permission slips passed around in our PE class.

"We're going to start our swimming unit in PE soon," said Coach Jenkins. "That means we'll start having PE in the community pool next to our school, instead of the gym. Be sure to tell your parents!"

All the kids in the class cheered.

"Yay, I love swimming!" said my best friend, Sally. "I can't wait to go to the pool during PE!"

Everyone seemed really happy about the news.

When she noticed that I wasn't smiling and cheering like everyone else, Sally asked, "What's wrong, Mindy? Do you not like to swim?"

I glanced around to check if anyone was listening and whispered so only Sally could hear, "I don't know how."

"*What?*" Sally looked shocked. "Did you not learn how to swim? We all learned when we were little!"

I shook my head. "We never learned how in my old school in San Francisco. We just always had PE at the gym! And my dad never signed me up for lessons or anything either."

"Oh . . ." Sally scratched her chin. "I guess that makes sense. Here everyone learns to swim pretty early, I think. Since we live so close to the beach

and all. But wait a minute. Isn't San Francisco also close to the beach?"

I nod. "Yeah, but the water is usually too cold to swim in it. The beaches there are different from the ones here. A lot of my friends at my old school didn't know how to swim either."

Sally wrinkled her nose. "That sucks. Well, the permission slip says that you don't have to participate if you don't know how to swim. Maybe you can do something else instead?"

"Maybe!" I nodded, but deep inside, I felt sad. I didn't want to be the only one in my class who wasn't in the water having fun during PE.

"It's also not too late for you to get swim lessons!" Sally added. "I think the beginner classes at the community pool are usually for little kids, but maybe you can join in!"

I perked up. "That's a great idea, Sally! I'm going to ask my dad if he can sign me up."

Maybe there was hope after all!

Chapter 2

Later that evening, my family and I sat at the table for dinner. Today we were eating bibimbap along with some dumplings that my new stepmom, Julie, had made. Since Dad and I are Korean and Julie is Chinese, we always try to eat food from both our cultures as much as we can.

Dad and Julie had recently gotten back from their honeymoon, so they still had tans. Dad especially looked pretty funny because he had white circles around his eyes from where he'd worn sunglasses!

Dad and I–and my dog, Theodore the Mutt–were

still getting used to having Julie live with us. I loved her, but she'd just moved in a few days ago, right after they got back from their trip. It was still weird to have another person in the house!

Dad and Julie seemed really happy, though, so I didn't mind. They were always smiling and laughing. I liked seeing Dad laugh so much! And Julie was nice to Theodore and me too.

At the beginning of dinner, Dad and Julie talked about something funny that had happened at work today. The two of them work at the same company. It's how they first met!

They laughed as they ate, and I smiled too, even though I had no idea what they were talking about. Sometimes it's easier to just pretend to know what other people are saying. Especially if they're adults.

But then Dad said, "How about you, Mindy? How was your day?"

Now was my chance! I ran to my room, got the

PE permission slip from my backpack, and showed it to Dad.

He put his chopsticks back down on his bowl so he could take the paper from me.

"Swimming in PE class!" he exclaimed when he read the paper. "That sounds fun! But Mindy, you don't know how to swim!"

I sadly shook my head. "Nope. All the other kids in my class know how, but I don't."

"That's so cool that you guys can swim for PE!" Julie said. "That's pretty rare. I guess your school is lucky since there's the community pool right next door."

"There's also that beach nearby, so I get why the school wants the kids around here to know how to swim," Dad added. He frowned and looked back at me. "Well, Mindy, maybe you can still participate with floaties on. Or stick to the shallow end! I'll email your teacher and we'll figure something out."

"Okay," I said.

Dad and Julie went back to eating, but I didn't go back to my spot at the table.

"Appa?" I asked. *Appa* is the Korean word for "Daddy."

"Hmm?" Dad replied, looking up from his food.

"All the other kids are going to make fun of me if I have floaties on. And even if they don't, I don't want to be the only kid in my class who can't swim. It'll be too embarrassing. Can I get swim lessons? Sally said that the community pool offers classes."

Dad glanced at Julie, who nodded. Dad turned back to me and shrugged. "I don't see why not!" he said. "Swimming is a valuable life skill. And it'd be fun if you could properly learn. Then we could go on a family snorkeling vacation in Key West during one of your school breaks! While we were away for our honeymoon, Julie and I actually talked about how we definitely want to go back there with you someday."

"It was *really* nice," Julie added. "We could

maybe even bring Theodore if we can find a pet-friendly hotel!"

We all looked at Theodore. He wagged his tail and barked with excitement.

A family vacation in Key West sounded like a dream come true!

"Thanks, Appa!" I said. "I'll work extra hard to learn how to swim!"

Chapter 3

On the first day of PE at the pool, Coach Jenkins brought me a kickboard and a pair of floaties.

"Your dad told me you don't know how to swim yet, Mindy," he said. "But if you still want to get in the water, you can with these. And I'll keep an eye out for you, and the community-pool lifeguards will too! Just be sure to stick to the shallow end, and try practicing moving around in the water. Hopefully, one of these days you can join your classmates in the lap lanes."

Besides me, there was only one other kid in our class who couldn't swim. I didn't know him too well other than the fact that his name was Charlie.

Charlie and I moved around in the shallow end with our floaties and kickboards while watching the other kids do laps in the pool. It stank. The water felt nice and warm, but I wished I could be swimming with my classmates.

To make things worse, we caught the attention of Brandon and his friends, a.k.a. the mean kids.

They looked at us and laughed.

"Look at those babies over there!" Brandon said. "They're nine like us but they can't even swim!"

Charlie and I glanced at each other. Charlie looked just as sad as I felt.

At the end of class, Sally tried to cheer me up.

"It's okay, Mindy," she said. "We can't all be good at everything."

"Yeah . . . ," I replied. "But I'm hoping I'll be able to swim soon! I asked my dad if I could take swim lessons, just like you suggested. And he said yes! I'm going to get really good at swimming.

Way better than Brandon and his friends!"

I must have said the last part too loudly, because Brandon heard and came over to where we were standing by the pool. With a mean smile on his face, he said, "Oh yeah? You wanna bet? Then why don't you race me one of these days? We'll see who's the best swimmer then—that is, if you can manage not to drown!"

Before I could respond, he and his friends walked away, laughing.

"Don't listen to him, Mindy!" Sally said. "You should focus on learning how to actually swim first. Racing someone when you're not ready is dangerous!"

I knew my friend was right, but I was still mad at Brandon. He was just so mean!

I clenched my fists. I was going to work hard during swim lessons and practice every day. I was going to become an expert at swimming. And then I was going to beat Brandon!

Chapter 4

Before my first swim lesson at the pool, Dad helped me put on my goggles.

The only pair of goggles in the house was Julie's. The goggles were a little too big for me, even when Dad tightened them all the way. They also had a weird tint that made the entire world look orange when I wore them. The color made me a little dizzy!

"Sorry this was the only thing we could find at the moment, kiddo," Dad said as we got out of the car. "We'll have to get you your own pair of goggles soon."

I was sad about the goggles, but I knew how lucky I was to be able to sign up for swim lessons so last minute. "It's okay, Dad. It's better than nothing."

When we got to the pool, I was really embarrassed to see that most of the kids in the beginner's class were way younger than me. They were around my baby cousin's age—like six! I scrunched up my shoulders, hoping that no one would make fun of me or ask why I was in this class.

Dad must have noticed I was embarrassed, because he said, "Sorry, Mindy. The class above this one, for older kids, seemed a bit too advanced, skill-wise, for you. Maybe we can move you up to that level once you've covered the basics here!"

"It's okay, Dad," I said again.

"Good luck!" Dad said. "I'll be watching from the bleachers."

"Thanks!"

I smiled and tried to keep a positive attitude as I approached the pool. But it was really hard,

especially when one of the little boys pointed at me and said, "What's she doing here? She's a big kid!"

The teacher, Ms. Wilson, replied, "Now, now, you're never too old to learn how to swim! Everyone here is actually still learning pretty early! Later this evening, I teach a swim class for adults!"

We all gasped. The little kids thankfully stopped staring at me after that.

Before any of us got into the water, Ms. Wilson had us do stretches and other warm-ups.

"It's super important to remember not to start swimming as soon as you get to the pool," she said. "It might make you feel self-conscious to hop around and stretch when everyone else is swimming, but we all need to spend some time warming up before we get in the water. Remember: safety first!"

When we were all done warming up, Ms. Wilson had us line up and sit along the edge of the shallow end of the pool. We dipped our feet in the water. It felt so nice!

"Okay," Ms. Wilson continued as she gave each of us a pair of floaties. "The most important thing to learn when you're starting off swimming is breathwork. Once we get in the water, what we're going to do is hold our breath to make a balloon face before we submerge our heads under the surface."

She got into the pool and then blew up her cheeks wide so she looked like a puffer fish! Then she stuck her face into the water. When she came back out, she opened her mouth with a "Pah!" sound.

It looked silly, but it looked kind of fun, too!

"Now you try!" Ms. Wilson said.

One by one, we got into the pool. When it was my turn, I made a balloon face and put my head in the water. Underneath the surface, everything was muffled. My goggles made everything look orange already, but down here they also made things look shimmery and bright.

After a few seconds, I lifted my head up again.

Like Ms. Wilson had done, I opened my mouth and said, "Pah!"

There were a lot of kids who got it on the first try like me. But some of the little ones weren't too happy. One kid even cried after putting her head underwater!

After making sure she was okay, Ms. Wilson told the rest of us, "Good! Now, let's try doing this a few more times."

We made balloon faces, put our heads in the water, and surfaced while saying, "Pah!" again and again.

"Okay, now, we're going to do the same thing but add bubbles this time!" said Ms. Wilson. "Make bubbles with your mouth for five seconds before coming up to say 'Pah!'"

By the time we finished, I felt really impatient. I'd signed up for this class to learn how to swim, not make bubbles!

I raised my hand.

"Yes, Mindy?" said Ms. Wilson.

"When are we going to learn actual swimming?" I asked.

Ms. Wilson smiled. "Probably not until the next class! Today we're going to focus on breathwork and floating on our stomachs. Both are essential to being safe in the water!"

I frowned. Breathing and floating didn't seem that important to me, but I trusted her. She was an expert, after all.

About halfway into class, Ms. Wilson took each of us, one by one, out into the water. She guided us out onto the surface with our arms spread wide and taught us how to float! When it was my turn, I was afraid I'd sink. Or drown! But then I remembered to blow my bubbles for five seconds and lift my head.

Soon I felt my body rise to the surface like it was supposed to.

"Excellent job, Mindy!" Ms. Wilson exclaimed. "You're making really good progress!"

Floating was not swimming, but it was cool to feel my body being lifted by the water. I was one step closer to becoming a swim champion—and beating Brandon!

Chapter 5

In the next few classes, we learned how to float more and properly move in the water. Soon I was ready to go up and down the shallow end on my own. Well, sort of. I still had a foam noodle in front of me, and Ms. Wilson was within arm's reach in case anything happened. But I was kicking by myself! And breathing correctly, too.

Focusing on holding my breath for five seconds before turning my head to take a breath on my side, I slowly but surely moved across the water.

"That's it, Mindy!" said Mrs. Wilson. "Now let's add our arms. It's okay if you forget to move them from time to time, but try lifting your arms one by one. Remember, up into the sky, back into the water, and to your side. Up into the sky, back into the water, and to your side."

To help myself remember to do everything, I counted as I kicked five times and lifted my right arm to take a breath. Then I did the same on my left side. *Up to the sky, back into the water, and to my side. Up to the sky, back into the water, and to my side.*

My head hurt a little from trying to remember all the steps, but it was still fun. Ms. Wilson had me go all the way to the opposite end of the pool and then back. By the third time, I didn't have to think about what my body was doing as much and could think more about other stuff!

As I swam, I imagined all sorts of funny things, like what would happen if Theodore jumped into the pool to swim with me, and how nice it would be to be able to swim with my friend Sally during PE.

Our house didn't have a pool, but Sally's did.

Maybe one day we could all go over to her house for a swimming party! And I could go on the snorkel trip at Key West with Dad and Julie. Or even swim with manatees and dolphins!

The little kids didn't have to do as many laps, but since she thought I was ready, Ms. Wilson had me do four laps total. By the last one, I was pretty tired, but it kept me going to think about all the fun I would have with my friends and family.

It was going to be a whole new world after I learned how to swim!

Chapter 6

After a couple more lessons, Ms. Wilson moved me to the higher-level class, where I could more quickly learn how to swim by myself. I was kind of scared, but I was also excited. Finally, I was with kids my age!

On my first day in the new level, I saw Lindsey, one of my friends from school. Lindsey and I had been in the same class together in third grade, but we were in different classes now, so I hardly saw her at school anymore. Still, I was so happy to see someone I knew that I gave her a big, friendly wave.

"Hey!" I said. "I didn't know you took swim

lessons too! I just got moved up from the class for little kids."

"Hi!" she replied, waving back at me. "Yeah, I do. I know the basics on how to float and all that, since my dad taught me for safety reasons, but I'm still not as good as the kids in school, so I'm here! I'm glad I'm not the only one who has to take classes. I never learned to swim much while I lived in Minnesota."

I laughed. "I'm glad too! I was getting lonely in the other class since all the other kids were babies. We didn't swim in my old school in San Francisco, either!"

Soon it was my turn to try swimming in the shallow end without the noodle.

"It's okay to stop swimming at any time and just stand if you feel like you need to, Mindy," Ms. Wilson reminded me. "But otherwise, remember to keep floating on your belly and continue moving your arms and legs."

I nodded. As excited as I was to finally swim on my own, I felt nervous. I could hear my heart pounding!

Previously, Ms. Wilson had stood nearby and guided me as I swam. But this time I was going to swim by myself with her just following me from behind. I really hoped I wouldn't panic or swim into anything.

When Ms. Wilson blew her whistle, I pushed forward into the water. I made sure to remember to keep kicking and moving my arms and breathing just the way she taught us.

Kick kick kick kick kick. Breathe! Kick kick kick kick kick. Breathe!

I was doing it! I was really swimming!

Thwack! Suddenly, I hit something! I resurfaced, only to find that I'd swum into one of the buoys that separated the shallow end from the deep end. A few of the other kids laughed when they saw what'd happened.

"Mindy!" exclaimed Ms. Wilson. "Are you okay? I blew my whistle to tell you to stop, but you just kept going!"

"Sorry!" I exclaimed. "I'm okay."

I was fine . . . just really embarrassed. I couldn't even look at where the other kids were standing by the steps of the pool.

I glanced back toward where Ms. Wilson was standing to see where I'd gone wrong. Instead of going straight, I had veered way off course and gone sideways!

I bent my knees so my head submerged back into the water. I wanted to hide somewhere. Fast!

"It's all right, Mindy! It happens," Ms. Wilson said. "Just please remember to look forward and watch where you're going, okay? Can you try swimming back toward me?"

I nodded.

I swam, and this time I focused my eyes on Ms. Wilson. Keeping straight was easier now that I

was paying attention to where I was going.

Thankfully, I didn't swim into anything.

When I returned to the back of the line, Lindsey lifted her hand for a high five.

"What's that for?" I asked, still feeling a bit sad.

"For doing a whole lap in the pool by yourself, silly! The rest of us have all done it before, but this was your first time, right?"

She was right! I'd been so embarrassed about swimming into the buoy that I'd totally forgotten my big accomplishment.

I high-fived Lindsey.

"Yeah! Go, us, for learning how to swim!"

Even though I knew I still needed to practice a lot more, I was really proud of Lindsey and me!

Chapter 7

The next day at school, I was able to swim in the shallow end during PE. I didn't think I needed it, but Coach Jenkins gave me a noodle tube so I could latch on to it if I ever wanted help.

So far, so good! I only grabbed the noodle once.

Charlie was swimming around the shallow end with me too, but unlike me, he was still fully holding on to the noodle.

I felt kind of bad that he couldn't take swim lessons like I did. I hoped he would be able to learn how to swim soon too! Luckily, we still had lots of fun together as we went around the pool.

Sally came over to talk to me when she was done with her laps. "Wow! You can actually swim by yourself now!"

"Yup!" I said. "I've been practicing lots. I still have a problem with going straight, but otherwise I'm pretty good!"

Sally laughed. "Oh yeah, it's really hard to keep straight, especially in the shallow end where there aren't any lines. Don't worry, it's much better in the lap lanes! Everything is clearly divided there."

At that moment, Brandon and his friends came to talk to us.

"Hey, Mindy!" Brandon said. "Are you ready to race me?"

I clenched my fists. I really wanted to race Brandon, and I was so close to being the swim champion I needed to be to beat him!

"Not yet!" I said. "But I'll be ready soon!"

Brandon laughed in a mean way. "Yeah, right.

You just don't want to admit you're too chicken to race me!"

I was about to yell back at Brandon when Coach Jenkins intervened.

"Now, now, Brandon, Mindy is trying her best to learn how to swim. She just got the hang of swimming by herself. We shouldn't rush her!"

"He's right!" Sally said. "It's not safe to rush people when they're learning an important skill like swimming. Back off, Brandon!"

Brandon harrumphed and went back to playing with his friends.

"Don't worry, Mindy," Sally said. "Soon you'll be so good at swimming that Brandon will regret ever challenging you. I believe in you!"

"Thanks, Sally!" I said. "I really am trying my best to learn how. Honestly, I'm kind of grateful for Brandon. He makes me so mad, and that makes me want to try harder!"

We laughed.

"That's one way of looking at it!" replied Sally. "You got this, Mindy!"

I gave her a big smile. I was so grateful to have a friend who believed in me like Sally did!

Chapter 8

That Friday, Dad and Julie surprised me by picking me up after school. Usually, my babysitter, Eunice, picked me up and stayed with me until they got home from work. But not today. Instead of being in their work clothes, Julie was wearing a sundress while Dad had on a T-shirt and shorts. And they had a change of clothes for me in the back seat!

Theodore licked my face when I got into the car. I gave him a big hug and sat him on my lap. I had no idea what was going on, but I was excited.

"Hey, Mindy!" Dad said. "You've been working so hard at school and with swim lessons. What do you say we take some time today to go have fun at the beach?"

"We finished the work we had to do for the week, so we left the office early today," Julie explained with a wink.

"That sounds perfect!" I said. "Thanks for the surprise, Dad! Thanks, Julie!"

Dad drove us to the beach by the school. I'd gone there plenty of times with my friends and family, but this was my first time going with Dad, Theodore, *and* Julie!

When we arrived, the sun was shining bright in the sky, and the sand was warm underneath my feet. After I got changed, we ran to the shoreline and started playing in the water, splashing one another, and having fun!

At first Theodore was scared of the water. He barked at each wave as it crashed onto the shore. But after watching us have so much fun, he wagged his tail and slowly walked into the water to join us!

I picked him up and gave him a hug.

"Good boy, Theodore! You're so brave!"

Soon afterward, we got hungry.

"Julie and I brought snacks from the Korean market!" Dad announced. "Let's take a break to eat something before we play some more."

"Okay!" I exclaimed. "Thanks for getting the snacks!" Dad and Julie were the best.

From a picnic basket, Dad brought out cans of Chilsung Cider and some gochujang-flavored shrimp chips. The red-pepper seasoning made the shrimp chips spicy, but they were so good!

"Wow, these are really delicious," Dad said. "I can't stop eating them!"

"Yeah, I like them a lot," I agreed. "They're my favorite!"

As Julie, Dad, and I happily munched away, I couldn't help but notice that Theodore was staring at us. I felt bad that we were eating yummy snacks without him.

"Dad, did you bring treats for Theodore?" I asked. "He looks so hungry and sad!"

"Yup, don't worry, Mindy. Let me grab some from the car. I'll also grab a ball so we can play fetch with him!"

Dad ran to the car and came back with a bright red ball and a bag full of peanut butter-flavored treats. He also returned with a familiar-looking girl and a Siberian husky puppy!

"Look at who I ran into in the parking lot!" Dad exclaimed.

It was my friend Lindsey! She looked happy and surprised to see me. Lindsey's dog yipped and pulled on the leash, trying to say hi to Theodore. Theodore wagged his tail and slowly approached the other dog.

"Hey!" Lindsey said to me. "What are you doing here?"

"We're here for a family beach day! How about you?"

"That's cool! I live nearby, so I always walk my

dog around the beach after school. This is Loki. She's four months old, so she's still a baby, but she's really friendly!"

I introduced Lindsey to Julie and Theodore. Julie gave her a big, friendly wave, while Theodore licked her hand.

Lindsey smiled and petted him on the head. "Mindy, your dog is so cute!" she exclaimed.

"Yours, too! I like her pretty blue eyes."

We all watched as Loki and Theodore played together. Even though Loki was only a few months old, she was already bigger than Theodore! She was very playful and kept pouncing around Theodore. Since the beach was pretty empty, we let the dogs go off leash and watched them run around and try to catch each other. They were really cute!

While we were watching the dogs, I let Lindsey try the shrimp chips. When she tasted one, she took a step back.

"Wow, this is really spicy!" she exclaimed.

"But . . . can I have some more?"

"Be careful," Julie said with a smile. "They're addicting!"

We all laughed.

After we finished eating, we took turns tossing the ball so Theodore and Loki could play fetch. Loki was bigger, but she was clumsier, while Theodore was small and fast! It was fun seeing which dog would get the ball.

Our afternoon had been good already, but it was more fun with a friend and another dog in the mix. In what seemed like no time at all, the sun started to set, so Dad, Julie, and I gave Lindsey and Loki a ride back home. On our way, we talked about school, swim lessons, and yummy food. Lindsey was really funny, and her jokes made us laugh so much.

It was the best beach day ever!

Chapter 9

That night, Dad and Julie came into my bedroom to say good night to Theodore and me. Usually it was either Dad or Julie who tucked me in, so it was nice having both of them here with me now.

Dad was hiding something behind his back.

"Mindy," he said, "I know you've been working really hard to learn how to swim. So Julie and I have something we'd like to give you."

He brought his hands forward to show me a small rectangular box.

I opened the gift. It was a pair of cute pink goggles!

"Sorry we didn't have goggles for you when you first started swimming," Dad said. "Julie and I wanted to get you the perfect pair, so it took us a while, but we hope you like them! You'll probably be able to see a lot better with these!"

I tried them on. They fit perfectly, neither too big nor too small. And the best part was, they weren't tinted, so they didn't make the entire world look orange!

"Thanks, Dad! Thanks, Julie!" I said. "I really love them!"

I gave them both a big hug. Afterward, Dad and Julie sat down on the bed.

"Mindy, did I tell you that I didn't learn how to swim until I was an adult?" Julie asked.

I gasped. "No, you didn't! Why did you learn to swim so late?"

"Well, I didn't grow up near a beach like you, so when I was a kid, I didn't really need to know how to swim. I don't think my parents ever learned either.

But then in college, we could choose anything as a PE elective. So I chose to learn how to swim! I felt like it was an important life skill to have."

"Was it hard for you to learn?" I asked.

"Yup. You're doing a lot better than I did, Mindy! I think it helps that you are super motivated. And you've grown up around water, so you're not afraid of it. When I was first starting out, I was really scared, so it was hard for me to even keep my head down in the water!"

"Really?"

"Yup, but I stuck through it, and by the end of the semester I was doing laps in the school pool all by myself!"

"That's amazing!" I said. "I'm so glad you didn't quit, Julie. Otherwise, how are we supposed to go swimming with manatees and dolphins together? Or go snorkeling?"

Dad and Julie laughed.

"Thanks, Mindy," Julie said. "I'm glad I didn't

quit either. It's important to overcome our fears! They can sometimes hold us back from making great memories with the people we love."

"Julie and I had so much fun swimming in Key West," Dad said. "I really hope we can all go together someday!"

"Me too!" I said.

"Even so, Mindy, I don't want you to put too much pressure on yourself," Dad added. "Swimming is a good skill to have, and we can't wait to do fun family activities with you, but the thing we want most of all is for you to be safe. It's so important to take as much time as you need to properly learn how to swim!"

"Don't worry, Dad," I said. "I'll take my time. I'll learn how to swim so we can go see the manatees! And the dolphins!"

We all laughed and pulled in together for another group hug.

Chapter 10

In PE on Monday, Coach Jenkins said, "Okay, class, this Friday, we're going to have a swimming test. It's not going to be anything scary, so don't worry. I just want to see how everyone is doing in terms of developing their swimming skills!"

I gulped. I knew I'd improved a lot since I'd first started swimming, but I hoped it would be enough!

"Today, though, we're going to have some free swim time. The only requirement for this class is that you keep moving. This is still PE, after all! The lifeguards and I will be watching to make sure everyone stays safe."

Coach Jenkins brought out swim rings and other fun toys that we could play with in the pool.

Sally came over to where I was in the shallow end.

"Hey, Mindy, since we have the test coming up, do you want to try racing me?" she asked. "It's okay if you don't feel ready yet, though."

"Yeah!" I exclaimed. "Sounds fun."

Even though I was nervous about Friday, I was excited to put my skills to the test. And Sally was my best friend, and she was nice, so I knew she wouldn't make fun of me if I lost.

We went to the far end of the pool, where there weren't a lot of people. Luckily, most of our class-mates were hanging out by the deep end.

"Let's try swimming to the opposite side," said Sally. "Feel free to stop whenever you need to, though. This is just for fun!"

"Okay! Thanks, Sally."

We hung at the side of the pool, our arms out-stretched in front of us.

"Ready . . . set . . . go!"

We took off, and I tried my best to go straight and keep my arms and legs moving. I kicked and kicked, but no matter how hard I tried, I couldn't catch up to Sally! She was just too good!

It seemed like she moved three times as much as I did whenever I kicked. It was like trying to swim against a mermaid!

Sally reached the other end of the pool when I wasn't even close. I wanted to finish swimming to the other side too, but I was too tired. So I stood up and waded through the water the rest of the way. When I reached her, Sally waved at me.

"I didn't even come close to beating you!" I said, disappointed in myself. "And I couldn't swim all the way, either."

"It's okay," Sally replied. "I learned how to

swim a really long time ago, when I was a baby! Meanwhile you *just* learned recently. It'd be weird if you beat me the first time you tried!"

I laughed. She was right. It *would* be weird if I beat Sally when I hadn't even been swimming for that long!

Coach Jenkins came over to stand beside where we were at the pool.

"Great improvement, Mindy!" he said. "Good job on stopping when you didn't feel comfortable continuing to swim. Thankfully, Friday's test won't be a race, so you won't have to rush yourself in any way. We'll be timing you, but it won't be a competition."

"That's a relief!" I exclaimed. "I'm probably the slowest kid in the class."

Coach Jenkins shook his head. "It's not good to compare yourself to others, Mindy. Remember, you're just starting out! We all learn at our own pace."

"Thanks for the reminder, Coach," I replied. "I'll try to keep that in mind!"

"No problem. You're doing great, kid!"

"Yeah, you totally are!" Sally grinned at me. "You should be proud of yourself!"

I nodded and grinned back at Sally. I felt so lucky to have such a nice friend like her!

Chapter 11

On Friday, Coach Jenkins had everyone in our PE class line up at the pool. After we all warmed up, he had the first three kids get into the water and spread out so they each had enough space in the shallow end.

I was glad I wasn't part of this group, but I was still super nervous because Sally, my best friend, was one of the first kids to swim. She didn't look that scared, though, probably because she knew she was a good swimmer. Sally was so awesome!

"Everyone will be swimming to the other end of the pool and back," Coach Jenkins said. "I will be timing everyone as they swim, but please remember *not* to rush. I'm just timing everybody so I can compare your times from now to the end of the semester. This is not a race!"

The kids in the water still looked a little nervous, and I could see why! Even if their times didn't matter, they were still being watched by everyone else in the class.

Coach Jenkins started the timer and said, "Go!"

The kids took off. Even though I knew it wasn't a race, I couldn't help but be proud of how much faster Sally was than anyone else in her group. I felt a lot better about losing to her too. No wonder she beat me so easily! I didn't think *anyone* in our class was as fast as her!

When she got out of the water, I gave her a high five. "You were so amazing!" I exclaimed.

"Thanks, Mindy!" Sally gave me a sheepish smile. "It's all because I grew up with a pool behind our house. Now that you can swim, you and Theodore should totally come over to swim with my sisters and me sometime!"

It was like Sally had read my mind! My dream of swimming with my best friend and our dogs was one step closer to becoming true. "That'd be so fun!" I said. "Thanks for inviting us, Sally!"

Too soon, Coach Jenkins said, "Okay, Mindy, you're up!"

It was my turn to swim! Before I could go into the pool, though, Brandon stepped in front of me and said, "Let's see how fast you can swim! I bet you can't beat *my* time."

"Leave her alone!" Sally said. "This is not a race."

"Yes, Brandon, please step aside and leave Mindy alone," Coach Jenkins agreed. "Today is not about competition; it's about personal improvement!"

Brandon harrumphed and stepped aside. "Fine, but don't think I forgot about our race!" he told me. "You still have to challenge me one of these days."

"Don't worry, I didn't forget," I replied. "Not a single bit!"

I was still a little nervous when I got into the water, but I bounced up and down a little bit to calm down. *This isn't a race!* I reminded myself. *I just have to do my best.*

When Coach said, "Go!" I swam and swam as best as I could. The other kids zoomed past me, but I focused on keeping a steady pace. Today I just wanted to be able to go to the other side of the pool and back without stopping like I'd had to when I raced Sally. Maybe if I thought less about winning and more about breathing, kicking, and everything else Ms. Wilson had taught us during swim lessons, I could make it!

When I got to the other end of the pool, I had to take a little break. The other kids just turned around and swam back right away, but I remembered what Coach had said about how important it was to not rush myself.

Sally was waiting for me when I finished my lap.

"You did it!" she exclaimed. "Good job."

"Yes, great job, Mindy!" said Coach Jenkins. "It's so good to see that you can make it all the way now."

"Thanks, Sally. And thanks, Coach Jenkins! It helped to not worry about how everyone else was doing compared to me."

Coach smiled. "I'm glad it was helpful! Even though it's true that you're not as fast as the other kids right now, speed is something that can easily be improved with more practice. Proper technique and safety are far more important!"

I nodded. It might take longer than I wanted, but I was determined to work hard to improve my speed so I could beat Brandon!

Chapter 12

When I finally felt more confident in my swimming, Sally told me about her great idea.

"I can have a pool party at my house and invite our friends, Brandon, and Brandon's friends! That way, if you win, we can celebrate with our friends! And if you lose, we'll be there to cheer you up!"

"Yeah!" I said. "We can still have fun at the party no matter what happens!"

"Yup! And our parents can be there too. To make sure everyone stays nice and safe."

I really liked Sally's idea. She was so smart!

"*Also*, my house is right by Signor Morelli's,"

Sally added. "So we can go there for dinner after the party!"

"Perfect!"

Signor Morelli's is the really good pizza restaurant in our neighborhood. I once got vouchers for free pizza from them because Dad, Julie, and I won our school trivia competition. Even though we go there a lot, I never get tired of it. Their pizza is *that* good!

We high-fived. I was nervous about swimming against Brandon, but I was glad I could finally go to a pool party at Sally's! Although I'd been to Sally's house a lot of times, I'd never gotten a chance to play in her huge pool before.

All our friends were super excited when we invited them to the party. Since Brandon wasn't my friend or Sally's, though, I was afraid he would say no when we invited him. But as soon as Sally mentioned that we were inviting a bunch of other people from our class, Brandon perked up.

"I'll be there!" He pumped his fist and then turned to me. "Wait, are we going to race at the party?"

"Yup! I've been practicing a lot."

Brandon raised an eyebrow. "Are you sure? And you won't cry like a baby when I leave you in the dust?"

I clenched my fists. Brandon always knew exactly what to say to make me mad. But I wasn't going to let him make me lose my temper.

"I won't cry," I said. "I'm going to beat you!"

"Yeah, yeah, just keep telling yourself that," Brandon said. "Do you want us to stick to the shallow end? Since you only recently learned how to swim and all."

I blinked. I was surprised that Brandon was being so thoughtful. Maybe he wasn't a complete poop face after all!

"Sure. Thanks, Brandon!"

He looked away. "There's nothing to thank me

for! If something happened to you at the pool, it'd be a real pain in the butt."

I rolled my eyes. Of course, he wouldn't be *that* nice!

"I don't want anything to happen to me, either," I replied. "So we're good!"

"I can't wait for everyone to see me beat you!" Brandon continued. "Get ready to lose big time on Saturday!"

I laughed and walked away, shaking my head. Sometimes Brandon was so mean, he was predictable!

"See you at the party, Brandon!"

The night before Sally's pool party, Dad came to tuck me in for bed. Both Dad and Julie were coming with me to the party tomorrow, but I hadn't told him yet about what was going on between me and Brandon.

I took a deep breath and told him about everything.

Dad looked mad when he heard about how Brandon had been teasing me. "I feel like this Brandon kid has been mean to you for a long time, and that's not okay. Do you need Julie and me to step in and tell him to stop? Maybe we can meet with his parents."

I shook my head. "Thanks for asking, but I can handle Brandon. We're going to race at Sally's party tomorrow to decide who's the better swimmer! I'll let you know if I need help, though."

"Okay . . . ," Dad said, looking unsure. "Well, I'll keep a close watch on him tomorrow to make sure he doesn't get out of hand. His parents are coming to the party too, right? I'm going to talk to them about what's been going on."

"I think so! And sounds good. Thanks for being there for me, Appa."

"Of course! Julie and I are always here for you, Mindy, no matter what. Never forget that."

"I won't!" I gave Dad a big hug. "I love you."

"Love you too."

Chapter 13

On the day of the pool party, Dad, Julie, Theodore, and I went to Sally's house. Being able to bring my dog was definitely one of the best parts of swimming at my friend's!

"We'll have to keep Theodore on a leash and be very careful, though, since we don't know yet if he can swim," Dad said. "I think a lot of dogs naturally can, but it's better to be safe than sorry!"

"Okay!" I said. "I'm just happy enough that we're bringing him to the pool!"

Sally's house is really big and nice. Even

though I've been to her house many times before, I'm always amazed by how huge it is!

We knocked on the door, and Sally gave us each a big hug when she let us in.

"Hey!" she said. "I'm so glad everyone could make it!"

I handed her a basket of Pepero, Choco Pie, and other Korean snacks on our way in. Since it's rude in Korean culture to show up to someone's house empty-handed, we'd gone to the Korean grocery store in the morning to get some yummy snacks.

"Wow, thanks, Mindy!" Sally exclaimed. "I'm sure everyone at the party will love these snacks!"

She led us to the back of the house, where a bunch of people were already gathered around the pool. Lindsey was there with Loki, and so were Brandon and some other kids from our school. I also saw Sally's older sisters, Patricia and Martha, and their parents, Mr. and Mrs. Johnson.

Happy music played from the speakers, and

everyone was laughing and having a good time. It was a fun family pool party!

Theodore was really happy to see Loki, and the two of them ran around each other the best they could with their leashes on.

After we said hi to everyone we knew, Dad and Julie went over to sit at the table where all the other parents were by the pool. I was expecting Brandon's parents to be there too, but instead I just saw an older kid who looked like Brandon. He was angrily talking to him about something when I walked over to them. Brandon looked sad, like the kid was saying something mean to him.

Before I could ask him what was wrong, though, Brandon said to me, "Finally! And I thought you'd be too chicken to show up."

I shook my head. "You can't get rid of me that easily!"

The older kid still looked mad, so I pointed at him and asked Brandon, "Who's he?"

"This is Blake," Brandon explained. "He's my older brother. Our parents were busy and couldn't make it, so they sent him to watch over me instead since he's eighteen."

"Hi, Blake! Nice to meet you!"

Blake turned his chin up and looked down his nose at me. He didn't even say hi back! I wondered if that was why Brandon was so mean.

Brandon and I walked over to where Sally was waiting for us by the pool.

"Okay," she said. "So the bad news is, there are a lot of people playing in the water right now. But the good news is, since our pool is different from the one at the community center, the water is shallow everywhere! That means you two can still race on the opposite side where there aren't that many people."

Sally pointed at the end of the pool that was farther away from us. Most of our friends were playing Marco Polo on the side closer to us, so there was still plenty of room for us to race!

"Cool," Brandon said. "I'm ready now if you are."

"Wait!" I replied. "We should warm up first. Just like we do in school."

Before we got in the water, Brandon and I both warmed up. I hopped around on one leg, and then the other. I stretched from side to side and lifted and lowered my knees. I wanted to be able to move as quickly and easily as I could without hurting myself!

When we were almost done stretching, Brandon and I looked around us to make sure everyone else was watching.

"Go, Mindy!" Dad cheered, and Julie and my friends joined in.

Brandon looked at my friends and family, and then at his.

His best friend, Mikey, cheered for him, but Blake was on his phone. And Brandon's other friends were too busy playing to pay attention to what was going on. Even though Brandon was mean to me, I still felt bad for him. I wished I could let him borrow some of my friends so they could cheer for him, too.

But at the same time, I was glad I had my friends and family. I was going to need all the support I could get to win this race!

"Okay," said Sally when we got into the water. She was going to be our referee. "So, you guys are going to do three laps. That's back and forth across the short side of the pool three times. Be sure to stay far enough away from the other person so you don't bother them. And remember, this is just for fun, so stop swimming if you feel tired or uncomfortable!"

She said the last part while looking at me. I nodded at her. I wanted to beat Brandon, but I was definitely going to be careful!

Brandon and I looked at each other.

"You ready?" he asked, giving me a mean grin.

"Yeah!" I replied. "Let's go!"

"Okay, then," Sally said. "Ready . . ."

I leaned forward and lifted my arm, preparing myself.

"Get set . . . go!"

Chapter 14

Brandon and I shot through the water. Even though I really wanted to look beside me to see how he was doing, I kept my attention in front of me and focused on my own breathing and swimming.

Kick kick kick kick kick. Breathe! Kick kick kick kick kick. Breathe!

Brandon pulled ahead of me. But instead of quitting like I did during my race with Sally, I kept my pace. My friends and family were loudly cheering me on from the bleachers. So even though I was losing, I still felt happy!

And then something unexpected happened.

Brandon lost his balance when he spun around for the last lap!

I sped past him, but then looked back to make sure he was okay. He was now standing in the water and hitting it with his fists. He seemed angry, but he didn't look hurt. I was about to go back to ask him if he was all right when he shot forward into the water.

Oh no! Brandon was trying to catch up!

I turned back around and swam and swam as fast as I could. My ears filled with the sounds of water splashing around us and the cheers coming from my family and friends.

I could do this! I really could do this!

I reached the end just seconds before Brandon did. I won!

"Mindy wins!" Sally exclaimed.

When I got out of the water, Sally and Lindsey gave me a hug. Dad, Julie, and Sally's sisters joined in too. Dogs can't hug, but both Loki and Theodore

leaped up and down and looked really excited.

I'd done it! I'd really beat Brandon!

I looked back at Brandon. He was all alone. His friend Mikey was playing with some other friends in the pool now, while Blake was still sitting at the parents' table and staring down at his phone.

I was happy I'd won, but I felt bad for Brandon, too. He looked so sad! And his brother hadn't even watched him swim like he was supposed to!

"Hey," I said, tapping him on the shoulder.

Brandon glared at me. "What do you want?" he asked. "You won, so now leave me alone."

I gulped. He was being mean, but I knew he was just upset he lost.

"My friends and I are going to Signor Morelli's for pizza after the pool party," I said. "Do you want to come? Mikey and Blake can come too, if they want."

Brandon blinked. He looked really confused.

"It's not a trick!" I quickly said. "I promise. I just

really love pizza! It makes everything better. It'd be my treat. I haven't used the free pizza voucher I got this month from the trivia competition yet!"

I expected Brandon to tell me to leave him alone again, but instead he slowly nodded. His shoulders relaxed, and then he *grinned* at me! And it wasn't a mean smile either!

"Okay, sounds fun. I love Signor Morelli's!"

"I do too!"

I was going to go back in the pool to play with Sally and Lindsey when Brandon said, "Don't think this is over yet, though. Just because we're going to get pizza together later doesn't mean I don't want a rematch. And next time I'm not going easy on you! Today I was just being nice because you're new at swimming."

Despite his not-so-nice words, he was smiling when he said that. And not in a mean way.

I laughed. "That's fine with me! Let's both try our best the next time we race!"

I held out my hand, and Brandon shook it with a grin. "Deal!"

Whether it was by winning against him in a race or by being nice to him, I'd finally beaten my worst enemy. And maybe . . . we were actually going to be friends!

After lots of practice, I'd successfully learned how to swim.

Now I just needed to make friends with manatees and dolphins!

Acknowledgments

Somehow, we've concluded yet another year of Mindy Kim books. Since it's only been a few months after *Fairy-Tale Wedding*, I don't really have any new people to thank. Rather than leave this space blank, though, I would like to again thank the readers, parents, teachers, librarians, and booksellers who continue to follow along with Mindy's adventures. Thank you so much for being Mindy's friends! She is so lucky to have a friend like you, especially in these peculiar, often scary times.

2021 was, personally and globally, a rough yet

strange year. Neither terrible nor good, but a big jumble of both. We saw the rise of scary amounts of division and violence. And there was a lot of confusion about how to proceed in these new "unprecedented" times. Yet, there were also sparks of good here and there that made us grateful for the people and things we have in our lives. I'm writing this in January of 2022, so I have no idea how the rest of this year will play out, but one thing I know for sure is that I will continue to write books that spread even just a bit more positivity in this world, and I thank you for reading and supporting my books as we try to figure everything out together. Because of you, reader, there will be more Mindy books after this year. And I am so grateful for that.

Continued thanks go to my agent, Penny Moore; my editor, Alyson Heller; my illustrator, Dung Ho; and everyone else involved in the making of the Mindy Kim books. Only the first two books came out during a pre-COVID world while the rest were released in times of great uncertainty and many changes, and yet somehow, here we are on Book Eight. Thank you for the love and hard work you've put into and continue to put into this series.

About the Author

Lyla Lee is the author of the Mindy Kim series as well as *I'll Be the One* and *Flip the Script* for teens. Born in South Korea, she's since then lived in various parts of the United States, including California, Florida, and Texas. Inspired by her English teacher, she started writing her own stories in fourth grade and finished her first novel at the age of fourteen. After working in Hollywood and studying psychology and cinematic arts at the University of Southern California, she now lives in Dallas, Texas. When she is not writing, she likes to watch K-dramas and play with her dog, Eiva the Siberian husky. You can visit her online at lylaleebooks.com.

Looking for another great book?
Find it
IN THE MIDDLE.

Fun, fantastic books for kids
in the in-be**TWEEN** age.

IntheMiddleBooks.com

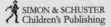